...along came Eric

For my mother

First published in Great Britain in 1991 by Andersen Press Ltd. This paperback edition first published in 1998 by Andersen Press Ltd., 20 Vauxhall Bridge Road, London SW1V 2SA. Published in Australia by Random House Australia Pty., 20 Alfred Street, Milsons Point, Sydney, NSW 2061. Colour separated in Switzerland by Photolitho AG, Gossau, Zürich. Printed and bound in Italy by Grafiche AZ, Verona.

10 9 8 7 6 5 4 3 2

British Library Cataloguing in Publication Data available.

ISBN 0 86264 856 4
This book has been printed on acid-free paper

...along came Eric

GUS CLARKE

Andersen Press
London

Everybody liked Nigel.

Nigel's family all liked Nigel

and, of course, all of Nigel's friends liked Nigel.

Father Christmas liked Nigel very much.

And, most of all, *Nigel* liked Nigel. (At least Nigel liked *being* Nigel, and that's just about the same thing.)

Then, along came Eric.

And it seemed to Nigel that suddenly nobody liked *Nigel* much anymore.

But everybody liked Eric a lot.

Nigel's family all liked Eric,

and all of Nigel's friends liked Eric.

Father Christmas seemed to like Eric very much indeed.

But sometimes Nigel wasn't sure that *Nigel* liked Eric...

...at all.

Years passed. Nigel grew up.

And so did Eric.

Nigel was surprised to find that nowadays everybody liked Eric *and* Nigel.

Nigel's family all liked Eric and Nigel (most of the time).

Nigel's friends still liked Eric, but Nigel didn't mind. Eric had friends of his own now and they all seemed to like Nigel as well.

Father Christmas? Well, he's a busy man, but he still found time to visit them...both.

And, best of all, Nigel liked Eric and Eric liked Nigel.
Very much.

"Life's not so bad," thought Nigel. (Eric had never thought it was.) But then...

...along came Alice.

More Andersen Press paperback picture books!

OUR PUPPY'S HOLIDAY
by Ruth Brown

SCRATCH 'N' SNIFF
by Gus Clarke

NOTHING BUT TROUBLE
by Gus Clarkee

FRIGHTENED FRED
by Peta Coplans

THE HILL AND THE ROCK
by David McKee

MR UNDERBED
by Chris Riddell

WHAT DO YOU WANT TO BE, BRIAN?
by Jeanne Willis and Mary Rees

MICHAEL
by Tony Bradman and Tony Ross

THE LONG BLUE BLAZER
by Jeanne Willis and Susan Varley

FROG IS A HERO
by Max Velthuijs